TONY HARI

A COLD COMING

ISBN: 1 85224 186 1 trade edition
1 85224 187 X limited signed edition

First published 1991 by
Bloodaxe Books Ltd,
P.O. Box 1SN,
Newcastle upon Tyne NE99 1SN.

Bloodaxe Books Ltd acknowledges
the financial assistance of Northern Arts.

ACKNOWLEDGEMENTS
These two poems first appeared in *The Guardian:* 'Initial Illumination' on 5 March 1991 and 'A Cold Coming' on 18 March 1991.

The cover photograph by Kenneth Jarecke was first published in *The Observer* and is here reproduced by kind permission of Popperfoto/Reuter: *'The charred head of an Iraqi soldier leans through the windscreen of his burned-out vehicle, February 28. He died when a convoy of Iraqi vehicles retreating from Kuwait City was attacked by Allied Forces.'*

Cover reproduction by V & H Reprographics, Newcastle upon Tyne.

Limited edition bound by DJB Bookbinders, Newcastle upon Tyne.

Printed in Great Britain by
E.F. Peterson & Son Ltd, South Shields, Tyne & Wear.

INITIAL ILLUMINATION

Farne cormorants with catches in their beaks
shower fishscale confetti on the shining sea.
The first bright weather here for many weeks
for my Sunday G-Day train bound for Dundee,
off to St Andrew's to record a reading,
doubtful, in these dark days, what poems can do,
and watching the mists round Lindisfarne receding
my doubt extends to Dark Age Good Book too.
Eadfrith the Saxon scribe/illuminator
incorporated cormorants I'm seeing fly
round the same island thirteen centuries later
into the *In principio*'s initial I.
Billfrith's begemmed and jewelled boards got looted
by raiders gung-ho for booty and berserk,
the sort of soldiery that's still recruited
to do today's dictators' dirty work,
but the initials in St John and in St Mark
graced with local cormorants in ages,
we of a darker still keep calling Dark,
survive in those illuminated pages.
The word of God so beautifully scripted
by Eadfrith and Billfrith the anchorite
Pentagon conners have once again conscripted
to gloss the cross on the precision sight.
Candlepower, steady hand, gold leaf, a brush
were all that Eadfrith had to beautify
the word of God much bandied by George Bush
whose word illuminated midnight sky
and confused the Baghdad cock who was betrayed
by bombs into believing day was dawning
and crowed his heart out at the deadly raid
and didn't live to greet the proper morning.

Now with noonday headlights in Kuwait
and the burial of the blackened in Baghdad
let them remember, all those who celebrate,
that their good news is someone else's bad
or the light will never dawn on poor Mankind.
Is it open-armed at all that victory V,
that insular initial intertwined
with slack-necked cormorants from black laquered sea,
with trumpets bulled and bellicose and blowing
for what men claim as victories in their wars,
with the fire-hailing cock and all those crowing
who don't yet smell the dunghill at their claws?

A COLD COMING

'A cold coming we had of it.'

T.S. Eliot
JOURNEY OF THE MAGI

I saw the charred Iraqi lean
towards me from bomb-blasted screen,

his windscreen wiper like a pen
ready to write down thoughts for men,

his windscreen wiper like a quill
he's reaching for to make his will.

I saw the charred Iraqi lean
like someone made of Plasticine

as though he'd stopped to ask the way
and this is what I heard him say:

'Don't be afraid I've picked on you
for this exclusive interview.

Isn't it your sort of poet's task
to find words for this frightening mask?

If that gadget that you've got records
words from such scorched vocal chords,

press RECORD before some dog
devours me mid-monologue.'

So I held the shaking microphone
closer to the crumbling bone:

'I read the news of three wise men
who left their sperm in nitrogen,

three foes of ours, three wise Marines
with sample flasks and magazines,

three wise soldiers from Seattle
who banked their sperm before the battle.

Did No. 1 say: God be thanked
I've got my precious semen banked.

And No. 2: O praise the Lord
my last best shot is safely stored.

And No. 3: Praise be to God
I left my wife my frozen wad?

So if their fate was to be gassed
at least they thought their name would last,

and though cold corpses in Kuwait
they could by proxy procreate.

Excuse a skull half roast, half bone
for using such a scornful tone.

It may seem out of all proportion
but I wish I'd taken their precaution.

They seemed the masters of their fate
with wisely jarred ejaculate.

Was it a propaganda coup
to make us think they'd cracked death too,

disinformation to defeat us
with no post-mortem millilitres?

Symbolic billions in reserve
made me, for one, lose heart and nerve.

On Saddam's pay we can't afford
to go and get our semen stored.

Sad to say that such high tech's
uncommon here. We're stuck with sex.

If you can conjure up and stretch
your imagination (and not retch)

the image of me beside my wife
closely clasped creating life...

(I let the unfleshed skull unfold
a story I'd been already told,

and idly tried to calculate
the content of ejaculate:

the sperm in one ejaculation
equals the whole Iraqi nation

times, roughly, let's say, 12.5
though that .5's not now alive.

Let's say the sperms were an amount
so many times the body count,

2,500 times at least
(but let's wait till the toll's released!).

Whichever way Death seems outflanked
by one tube of cold bloblings banked.

Poor bloblings, maybe you've been blessed
with, of all fates possible, the best

according to Sophocles i.e.
'the best of fates is not to be'

a philosophy that's maybe bleak
for any but an ancient Greek

but difficult these days to escape
when spoken to by such a shape.

When you see men brought to such states
who wouldn't want that 'best of fates'

or in the world of Cruise and Scud
not go kryonic if he could,

spared the normal human doom
of having made it through the womb?)

He heard my thoughts and stopped the spool:
'I never thought life futile, fool!

Though all Hell began to drop
I never wanted life to stop.

I was filled with such a yearning
to stay in life as I was burning,

such a longing to be beside
my wife in bed before I died,

and, most, to have engendered there
a child untouched by war's despair.

So press RECORD! I want to reach
the warring nations with my speech.

Don't look away! I know it's hard
to keep regarding one so charred,

so disfigured by unfriendly fire
and think it once burned with desire.

Though fire has flayed off half my features
they once were like my fellow creatures',

till some screen-gazing crop-haired boy
from Iowa or Illinois,

equipped by ingenious technophile
put paid to my paternal smile

and made the face you see today
an armature half-patched with clay,

an icon framed, a looking glass
for devotees of "kicking ass",

a mirror that returns the gaze
of victors on their victory days

and in the end stares out the watcher
who ducks behind his headline: GOTCHA!

or behind the flag-bedecked page 1
of the true to bold-type-setting SUN!

I doubt victorious Greeks let Hector
join their feast as spoiling spectre,

and who'd want to sour the children's joy
in Iowa or Illinois

or ageing mothers overjoyed
to find their babies weren't destroyed?

But cabs beflagged with SUN front pages
don't help peace in future ages.

Stars and Stripes in sticky paws
may sow the seeds for future wars.

Each Union Jack the kids now wave
may lead them later to the grave.

But praise the Lord and raise the banner
(excuse a skull's sarcastic manner!)

Desert Rat and Desert Stormer
without scars and (maybe) trauma,

the semen-bankers are all back
to sire their children in their sack.

With seed sown straight from the sower
dump second-hand spermatozoa!

Lie that you saw me and I smiled
to see the soldier hug his child.

Lie and pretend that I excuse
my bombing by B52s,

pretend I pardon and forgive
that they still do and I don't live,

pretend they have the burnt man's blessing
and then, maybe, I'm spared confessing

that only fire burnt out the shame
of things I'd done in Saddam's name,

the deaths, the torture and the plunder
the black clouds all of us are under.

Say that I'm smiling and excuse
the Scuds we launched against the Jews.

Pretend I've got the imagination
to see the world beyond one nation.

That's your job, poet, to pretend
I want my foe to be my friend.

It's easier to find such words
for this dumb mask like baked dogturds.

So lie and say the charred man smiled
to see the soldier hug his child.

This gaping rictus once made glad
a few old hearts back in Baghdad,

hearts growing older by the minute
as each truck comes without me in it.

I've met you though, and had my say
which you've got taped. Now go away.'

I gazed at him and he gazed back
staring right through me to Iraq.

Facing the way the charred man faced
I saw the frozen phial of waste,

a test-tube frozen in the dark,
crib and Kaaba, sacred Ark,

a pilgrimage of Cross and Crescent
the chilled suspension of the Present.

Rainbows seven shades of black
curved from Kuwait back to Iraq,

and instead of gold the frozen crock's
crammed with Mankind on the rocks,

the congealed geni who won't thaw
until the World renounces War,

cold spunk meticulously jarred
never to be charrer or the charred,

a bottled Bethlehem of this come-
curdling Cruise/Scud-cursed millenium.

I went. I pressed REWIND and PLAY
and I heard the charred man say: